Every new generation of children is enthralled by the famous stories in our Well Loved Tales series. Younger ones love to have the story read to them. Older children will enjoy the exciting stories in an easy-to-read text.

British Library Cataloguing in Publication Data
Southgate, Vera
    The magic porridge pot – Rev. ed.
    I. Title   II. Gordon, Mike
    III. Series
    823′.914[F]
    ISBN 0-7214-1208-4

Revised edition

Published by Ladybird Books Ltd Loughborough Leicestershire UK
Ladybird Books Inc Auburn Maine 04210 USA

Printed in England

The Magic Porridge Pot

retold for easy reading
by VERA SOUTHGATE M A B Com
illustrated by MIKE GORDON

Ladybird Books

Once upon a time, there was a
poor widow, who lived with her
little girl. One day they had
nothing left in the house to eat.
The little girl ran off to the woods.
She sat down under a tree and
began to cry. She was so hungry!

An old woman came along and asked her why she was crying.

"Because I am so hungry," said the little girl.

The old woman gave the little girl a small cooking pot. "Take this," she said. "It's magic!

"When you are hungry, just say to the pot, 'Cook, little pot, cook!' and the pot will cook you some very good porridge.

"When the porridge is cooked,"
said the old woman, "you must
say, 'Stop, little pot, stop!'"

The little girl wanted some porridge
right away, so she said to the pot,
"Cook, little pot, cook!"

And each time the magic porridge
pot would cook some good, hot
porridge.

To her surprise the cooking pot began to cook some porridge! It smelt so good that she could hardly wait to try some.

When the porridge was cooked, the little girl said, "Stop, little pot, stop!" Then she ate every last bit of porridge.

The little girl ran all the way back home. She showed her mother the cooking pot and told her what the old woman had said.

Her mother was very pleased. "Now all our worries are over," she said, happily.

15

And her mother was right.

Whenever they were hungry they

said, "Cook, little pot, cook!"

One day the little girl went out for a walk. While she was out, her mother felt hungry, so she picked up the magic porridge pot and said, "Cook, little pot, cook!"

The magic pot did as it was told. The little girl's mother helped herself to a big plate of porridge and began to eat.

She was so busy enjoying the porridge that she forgot to tell the magic pot to stop cooking.

The pot went on and on, cooking more and more porridge.

23

Soon the porridge began to spill over the top of the magic pot.

When the mother saw what was happening, she knew that she should tell the magic pot to stop cooking. But she had forgotten the words!

The magic pot just went on and on, cooking more porridge. Soon there was porridge all over the table and all over the kitchen floor.

And still the magic pot went on cooking more and more porridge!

Soon the whole house was full of porridge.

And still the magic pot went on cooking more and more porridge!

Soon all the houses in the street
were full of porridge.

And still the magic
pot went on
cooking more
and more
porridge!

31

Soon almost all the streets in the
town were full of porridge.

And still the magic pot went on
cooking more and more porridge!

The people of the town ran out of their houses into the streets.

"Oh, dear!" cried the mother. "I can't remember how to stop my magic pot cooking more porridge."

The people were worried that soon the whole world would be filled with porridge!

Just as the porridge reached the
last house in the town, the little girl
came back from her walk.

She could hardly believe her eyes
when she saw all that porridge!

Her mother ran up to her and cried,
"Please tell the magic pot to stop
making more porridge!"

The little girl took the magic pot
from her mother and said, "Stop,
little pot, stop!"

And, at last, the magic pot stopped
cooking porridge.

But, if you ever want to visit that town, you will have to eat your way through an awful lot of porridge!

TONI'S
MENU
LARGE PORRIDGE
2.00
SMALL PORRIDGE
1.00
MED PORRIDGE   1.50
EXTRA'S...
BOWL 10p SPOON 5p